The Customer Service Your Customers Expect

Stories About Customer Service

Brenda Robinson & Harley Robinson

Order this book online at www.trafford.com
or email orders@trafford.com

Most Trafford titles are also available at major online book retailers.

Print information available on the last page.

ISBN: 978-1-4907-9898-1 (sc)
ISBN: 978-1-4907-9903-2 (e)

Trafford rev. 01/09/2020

www.trafford.com

North America & international
toll-free: 1 888 232 4444 (USA & Canada)
fax: 812 355 4082

Contents

Chapter 1

I Couldn't Have Been Speeding That Much

I was driving on a prairie highway. It was the middle of June in the middle of the day. The highway was clear and there was little traffic.

I had the windows rolled down and the tunes turned up. I was enjoying seeing the baby calves in the pastures and the farmers in the fields. I was in my own zone.

Then, I spotted the police car in the approach on the side of the road. My immediate thoughts went to, "*Was I speeding?*" My secondary thought was, "*I was probably speeding.*"

However, like most people in a difficult situation I deflected responsibility and looked for blame and defense.

"What's he doing out here in the middle of the day?"

"He is probably sitting there on his phone."

"Doesn't he have anything better to do then and sit out in the country - there could be real criminals, committing real crimes right now!"

"Maybe he was sleeping and didn't even see me go by?"

However, none of that helped!

The lights on top of the car turned on and he raced out behind me. *"Oh no! Now I'm going to get a speeding ticket"* was all I could think.

I am, by nature, a law-abiding citizen. So, as he raced up behind me, I pulled over. I felt fortunate that there was a truck pull out zone on my right and I pulled into it and stopped. He pulled in behind me.

I'm still mumbling to myself about not having time for this and how long it will take. I'm also getting myself ready to defend! I got my license, insurance and registration ready to present with my argument and defense.

"I wasn't speeding that much - I never passed anybody."

"The roads are clear, there is no traffic - what is the problem here?"

"I am in a bit of a hurry. I have an appointment in an hour."

I was watching in the rear-view mirror as he got out of his car and approached. I remember thinking that I have been driving longer than this kid has been alive. He is probably brand new on the job. I don't need a speeding ticket from some "young whippersnapper" who is trying to make points. My mood was not improving. I'm ready for an argument.

When he came to my window, he caught me completely by surprise. His first words stopped me in my tracks. He said, "First of all, can I just say thank you to you for pulling over so safely and quickly?" What could I say to that? My resolve dissolved, and I said with a smile, "Oh, that's okay."

He saw that I was holding my license, insurance and registration and quickly said, "I see you have all your documentation ready for me. Would it be alright if I took a closer look at your license and registration?"

He held my license out in front of him and looked at it for a moment. Then he said, "Oh, Brenda Robinson from Sherwood Park. Do you prefer to be called Brenda, or is it Mrs. Robinson?"

I paused for a moment. I thought I would try a little humour. I said, "You should probably call me Brenda. I didn't star in the movie or get to sleep with Dustin Hoffman."

With a look of confusion, he asked, "Who is Dustin Hoffman?"

I quickly realized that we were from different eras and different generations. It was not going to be easy to get him onside with our common understanding. I was flustered. I quickly explained with, "Oh, I forgot how young you are. That was a classic movie from years ago. It was called The Graduate. It starred Dustin Hoffman and Anne Bancroft. It was a movie about a love affair between an older woman and a younger man." I realized that I was babbling. He said, "Well I don't remember the movie and I'm not sure who those people are. But I am a fan of Paul Simon. On my playlist, I have a song called "Mrs. Robinson." Is there any connection?"

I jumped in with excitement, "That's it!" "That is the song from the movie. That's what I was referring to."

He answered with, "I like that song."

I was thinking, *"I like this kid because he likes my kind of music."* I told him that the song was also a classic and was sung by Simon and Garfunkel.

He seemed quite interested and said, "I'll pay closer attention the next time that goes by on my playlist."

My defense has disappeared, and I'm engaged in discussion instead.

He quickly went on by asking, "Would it be okay if I ask another question?

My reply was, "Of course, go ahead."

So, he asked his next question, "Do you travel this highway often?"

I responded with, "Yes I do - I'm certainly on this highway every few weeks."

Then he said, "Well then what I'm about to tell you about why I'm out here, you probably already have some awareness of. Last year on this stretch of highway we had two fatal accidents. Both, we believe, were related to speeding. So, I'm out here for very good reasons. I just want to slow people down. Get them home safely. Prevent those kinds of accidents. And, help people be more aware of their speed."

I listened carefully and then responded with, "Thank you!"

I've just said thank you to a police officer who is about to give me a speeding ticket. That was not in my plan for defense. What happened?

He came back with another question, "Were you aware that the maximum speed on this secondary highway is 100 kilometres per hour?"

I assured him that I was aware.

He then told me, "According to my radar device, you were travelling 123 kilometres per hour."

I really wanted to argue. I expected him to say, "You were speeding." Then I could argue. But it's hard to argue with travelling. I was indeed travelling.

I said, "I couldn't have been going that fast - I never passed a single car. I don't think I was going that fast. Are you sure?"

His reply was not what I was expecting. He said, "I get it. It is a beautiful day - you were probably enjoying the drive. Maybe you had the window down and the tunes turned up. This highway is clear and clean, maybe you just weren't paying attention to your speed. It's easy to get going too fast when that happens."

How can I argue? He is saying what I was saying, and I think he understands. I replied with, "I guess that's what happened. I just didn't realize I was going that fast."

He came back with the same explanation. He said, "But you know why I'm out here. I just want to slow people down. Get them home safely. Prevent accidents. And help people be more aware of their speed. I think I have already accomplished that last part."

I quickly said, "You have, I will definitely pay closer attention from now on."

He went on with, "So, that qualifies you for a ticket for $309.

I don't usually think that I "qualify" for this kind of news and I started with, "You are kidding, aren't you? That is an exorbitant amount to charge. Nothing happened - nobody was impacted."

He agreed and said, "You know, people are always shocked at how quickly the price of the ticket goes up after you exceed the 120 kilometres per hour mark. I understand that. So, what I'm going to do is reduce it to the next level which qualifies you for a ticket of $169."

I'm happy to qualify for this ticket. In fact, I quickly said, "Thank you so much!"

His response was that he could clearly see that I understood why he is giving me the ticket.

I said, "Of course I do."

I just realized that I have now thanked him twice for the speeding ticket he is about to give me. This was not in my original plan.

After that, he said to me, "I'm going back to my car to prepare your ticket. It will take me 10 or 12 minutes to get it ready. Are you okay waiting here?"

My reply was, "I'll be just fine - take your time."

What happened to that cranky old lady who was in a hurry and had an appointment? What a change!

He returned in less than 10 minutes. His first comment was, "Thank you so much for waiting patiently."

I replied with, "Thank you for being so quick."

He then asked, "Could I just take a few minutes to explain to you the options you have for looking after this ticket?"

I don't think I've ever thought of a speeding ticket with options attached. He held my ticket out for both of us to look at. He said, "you know you can always pay this ticket with a cheque in the mail."

I nodded.

"Or," he said, "You could come into this address and pay in person. We are always happy with that."

He went on, "Right now, we are piloting an online payment system. You can go to this website and follow the prompts. It can be paid immediately with a credit card. It only takes a few minutes to complete."

"Of course," he said, "You can certainly appeal this ticket. The steps for appeal are listed on the ticket."

When he finished with the options, I thanked him again. I just can't quit saying thank you for this ticket!

Then he asked, "Just out of my own curiosity, how do you plan to take care of this ticket?"

I hesitated and replied, "I'm not sure - I may look at the online option."

I can hardly believe I am engaging in a discussion about paying my ticket. That has never happened to me before. I have been told in the past that there would be a penalty for not paying in 30 days. This is a much different experience. My whole plan for defence has never been implemented.

As I put my documents away, he asked one more question, "Could I ask a favour?"

My reply was, "For sure."

He went on with, "Will you drive safely the rest of the way home and could you use your cruise control to help out with awareness?"

I agreed to do so and in fact, I did it. When I got home, I shocked myself with my follow up action. I actually went online and paid for the ticket. It may be the first time in my driving career That I have done that. I usually like to wait it out as long as possible and send payment resentfully at the last moment.

My short-term behaviour has changed. But, that's not all. I still travel that same prairie highway. And, I don't speed on that highway. I wouldn't want to meet that same young officer and disappoint him.

What a difference a positive approach can make! What were the customer service strategies that impacted this experience?

1. **Get off to a good start**
   Customers have developed their first impression within 45 seconds whether it is on the phone, in person or even by e-mail. Openings are a critical element of excellence in customer service.

2. **Demonstrate empathy and avoid apology**
   Minimize apologies and expressions which make the situation sound bad or unfortunate. When people hear "I'm sorry," or "unfortunately," they do not expect to get any good news in what follows. However, when people feel heard and understood they want to work with us. Together we can get best results.

The Importance of Empathy

In customer service, customers want to be heard and they want to be understood. Empathy is sometimes confused with sympathy. Customers do not want you to feel sorry for them. They want you to understand their situation and work with them to find resolution. That is true empathy.

Empathy can be demonstrated in a number of ways:

1. **Shared experience:**
   "I've had something similar happen to me…"

   "There have been a number of people give us feedback on how that could be handled differently."

   "I talked to someone today who was dealing with the same situation…"

2. **Affirmation:**
   "You're right - that would not be helpful…"

   "That's correct. Those notices were sent out without checking the status of accounts."

   "Your description of the situation is clear and understandable…"

   "You are absolutely right to call and get more information…"

3. **Recognition for effort being made:**
   "Thank you for getting all of your statements ready before calling. That helps a lot."

   "You've done a lot of work to get all this information before calling us. Good work!"

   "Thank you for taking the time to call and discuss this situation with us."

   "You've done the right thing to have all of the amounts written down with dates. That helps a lot."

4. **Confirmation of understanding:**
   "Yes, I see it right here in your account. Thanks for pointing that out."

   "You are right - the payment was made the day after the notice was sent. I'm glad you are letting us know."

   "You are perfectly within your right to let us know when we can make a change or a correction. We appreciate it and it will be corrected."

5. **Focus on the action plan:**
   "Your account will be updated today. Just call if you receive another notice. It will be cancelled."

   "I put a note in your file that you have looked after that concern. You can call me at ____________, if you hear anything else."

Note:

Phrases like, "I understand," are not as effective as they once were. these phrases are sometimes received as condescending or patronizing. Some customers think they are being placated rather than "responded to."

3. **Connect on a personal basis**
   We are living in a world of connectedness. When people find common ground, it is the foundation for working better together.

4. **Ask instead of tell**
   Learn to ask more questions and do less "telling." Customers today would rather be asked than told.

When you ask questions, people feel involved, included and engaged. Questions suggest shared information. Questions stimulate action and often lead to shared solutions.

Questions also get customers thinking. Thinking or "rational" behaviour is much easier to work with than emotional behaviour.

5. **Explain why**
   We now live in a society where people expect to know why. They will ask why, and we have to be willing to explain why. Once they understand why, they will often be more willing to move on and accept the information at hand.

   This is particularly important when we are explaining policies, procedures, decisions and actions. Indeed, we should be proactive and prepare our explanations in advance.

6. **Focus on what can be done instead of what can't be done**
   Remember, people don't phone, email or come to your organization to find out what they can't do or what you don't do. We need to be willing to share information that helps customers understand what we can do and what is available to them.

   When we emphasize positive action, it is difficult for people to be disagreeable or difficult.

7. **Talk about what's next instead of what's past**
   Help customers get focussed on what's next. It is impossible to "undo" what has already happened. It is best to just get everyone focussed on moving ahead and looking for positive outcomes.

8. **Offer choices options and alternatives**
   When a customer is presented with options, choices and alternatives, the focus turns to thinking about action

instead of reaction. Achieving action is one of the keys to excellence in customer service.

Sometimes, we just need to get customers thinking about what else can be done. Our customers today are used to having choices. There are choices in all aspects of life. Children today are given choices. The marketplace is based on options. People seek out alternatives for almost everything they do.

When things are going reasonably well, we can offer two choices and most customers will respond. If anger or negative emotion is involved, we may need to offer three options. This is called the "tri-choice" approach. Sometimes we also need to use a forced choice. Offer the choices three times to positively push the customer to make a positive choice based on the alternatives.

9. **Move from formal to friendly**
   In all of our communication today. The tone has become less formal and more friendly. When we use phrases like, "Please be advised." Or, "It has come to my attention." We create a tone of formality. In customer service, people today are looking for a friendly tone.

10. **Manage vocabulary**
    Choose your words carefully. Excellence in customer service requires an awareness of negative trigger words and positive words to replace them.

Words to Avoid:	**Words to Emphasize:**
✕ Regret	✓ Yes
✕ Sorry	✓ Good
✕ Apologize	✓ Better
✕ Unfortunately	✓ Best
✕ Can't	✓ Progress
✕ Won't	✓ Action
✕ Couldn't	✓ Solution
✕ Shouldn't	✓ Success
✕ Didn't	✓ Excellent
✕ Don't	✓ New
✕ Fail	✓ Can
✕ Never	✓ Can do
✕ Reject	✓ Will
✕ Neglect	✓ Next step
✕ Deny	✓ Option
✕ Decline	✓ Choice
✕ Delay	✓ Could
✕ Trouble	✓ Would
✕ Problem	✓ Improved
✕ Difficulty	✓ Enhanced
✕ Inconvenience	✓ Answer
✕ But	✓ Assure
✕ Unable	✓ Positive
✕ Unavailable	✓ Decision
✕ Complaint	✓ Approach
✕ Impossible	✓ Alternative

Some people have said that this isn't really customer service. You bet it is. We are working together for best results. That is customer service.

Chapter 2

How Long Have You Been Waiting?

I walked into my bank. I never go to the bank anymore. Everything is online. My nearest approach to the bank would be an ATM. I was feeling resentful that I had to go into the bank for a simple transaction, but I had already tried to do it online and on the phone. They said it had to be handled personally in the bank. So here I was - walking into the bank reluctantly at best!

As soon as I entered, I saw a lineup of about 10 to 15 customers. At first, I felt some annoyance with my fellow customers. Why are they in the bank - why don't they handle this online or at the ATM. I chided myself for assuming that and reminded myself that there are things that can't be done that way.

Then I proceeded to incite negativity with others in the lineup. I asked the man in front of me in line, "How long have you been waiting?" He sounded annoyed and complained that he had been waiting for more than five minutes and hadn't moved.

The lady ahead of him chimed in with the comment that she had been waiting at least ten minutes without moving at all. We agreed that this situation is ridiculous. Two other people joined the chorus of complaints.

Then, I started to weigh in on which customer service representative I wanted to receive service from. The one on the right was someone I recognized as having worked in the bank for years. I had always assumed that she didn't really like the work and I was surprised to see she was still doing it. At one point she looked up and saw us all waiting in line. She rolled her eyes and said loudly to the customer in front of her, "I don't know what's going on today. Look at that lineup. I'm sure some of those people could use the ATM if they took the time to learn. Some people just won't get with the times."

I was shocked. It was okay for me to assume. I was not ok at all with her assumptions. I was acting very much like the offended customer and I was not happy.

Each time she finished with a customer she would turn to the line and loudly demand, "Next."

Now people in the line were talking about how rude her approach was. I started to make my plan. I was willing to trade with the person in front of me to avoid having to deal with her.

The customer service representative on the far left was almost the extreme opposite. She was so quiet and so timid we could hardly hear her. In her tiny sing song voice, she kept calling out, "I can help you over here. Would you like to come down here? Hello! I can help."

When she finally got a customer's attention, she could be heard complaining in a whiny voice, "I'm so sorry you had to wait. I don't know why we're so busy. You would think some of the managers would come out and help us when we are busy like that."

I recognized her attempt at empathy but found myself impatient with her approach. I couldn't see the value in blaming others for the situation. I decided that I didn't have the time or patience for the negativity.

This left me with no choice. I would have to deal with the young trainee in the middle! I was worried that my service need would not be something she was familiar with. I'll be honest, I often avoid trainees in fear that they will be slow or not knowledgeable. However, this was a choice I was happy to make. I had been watching and listening.

Every time she finished with a customer, she would look to the line, smile and say, "Come on down." We chuckled at the recognition of a familiar line from a television game show. Her lighthearted approach set a positive tone. When we arrived at her counter there was no complaining, whining or blaming. She simply said, "Thanks for waiting patiently, what can I do?"

Her approach was so efficient that she was handling more customers than her co-workers. Was it the difference in customer needs – maybe. It could also be the difference in service approach and attitude. She had completely moved from formal to friendly. She was aware of getting off to a good start. She didn't waste time apologizing or blaming. She provided excellent customer service.

She indeed had to ask for help to handle my request and she did it all with ease. She ended by thanking me for taking the time to come in personally. I didn't feel like I was causing a problem. I personally felt well served in a positive, productive way.

What were the customer service strategies that impacted this experience?

1. **Get off to a good start**
2. **Focus on what can be done instead what can't be done**
3. **Connect on a personal basis**

4. **Demonstrate empathy and avoid apology**
5. **Manage vocabulary**
6. **Move from formal to friendly**

What are the components of getting off to a good start?

1. Update your opening face to face statements. Customers have learned to respond in robotic ways to our old-style greetings. Consider replacements for the following:

   May I help you?
   How may I help you?
   Welcome to …

2. Update your openings for emails too! Old formal openings may not engage readers. Consider replacements for the following:

   Please be advised…
   This is to inform…
   Please find enclosed…
   We wish to inform…
   On behalf of…

3. Understand the importance of personalization. Offer and display your name and the name of your department. Extend your hand and greet each individual personally and in a directed way. Have business cards and info sheets ready for the customers. Vary your greetings to ensure attentiveness.

4. Manage the first 8 words in all of your communication.

Chapter 3

All Flights Are Cancelled

Airports are great places to see customer service at its best and at its worst. Indeed, sometimes you can see the best customers and the worst customers all in one setting.

I was at Toronto's Pearson Airport one day and saw it all happen. We were already at the gates. In many customers' minds, the stress is over. They have reached the airport, checked in, passed through security and are now waiting to board the flight to their destination.

On this day, there is lots of buzz in the waiting area about the weather. Many people are describing challenging drives to the airport. Snow is falling and there is talk of an impending blizzard. There are a few flight delays on the board, but most flights are still leaving after de-icing. Most travellers are optimistic. The storm seems to be local and conditions are still not too serious.

As darkness takes over, the tension builds. There are a few more delayed flights announced. Then the dreaded announcement comes over the PA system.

"All Air Canada flights are cancelled due to weather uncertainty. Out of concern for the safety of everyone, we will re-book all passengers for travel tomorrow. Please go to the customer service desk close to gate 22 to re-book your flight for tomorrow."

The rush for the customer service desk could be described as a stampede!

There may even have been some racing for position and some butting into line. The situation has changed dramatically from patient waiting to negative and demanding behaviour.

There are two service agents at the counter. There are no lineup ropes and people begin to line up in front of each agent. They are both getting their computers ready to process customer requests for re-booking. The young woman is having trouble with her computer and her non-verbal behaviour is of frustration and annoyance. She, at one point, throws her hands in the air and shrugs her shoulders. She's getting very angry with the slowness and her computer's unwillingness to respond.

Her co-worker, a young man, is also working to get his computer ready. He paused mid stream and called out to the lineup, "No worries folks - we are doing our best to get ready to respond to your requests. Thank you for your patience."

Indeed, he does this again after 3 or 4 minutes as he waits for his computer to respond.

After what seems like an eternity, the young woman and her computer are ready. She turns to the first person in line and says, "May I help you?"

Oh my, that good old question just seemed to backfire.

The customer in front of her answered harshly, "I hope somebody can help. Isn't that what you're paid to do? The decisions so far have certainly not helped. So - go ahead - help me."

The service agent was shocked. She responded with an apology. She said, "I'm sorry you're upset but there is nothing we can do about the weather. Let's move on - how can I help you?"

The apology didn't seem to help either. The customer seemed to have gained purpose as he raised his volume and said, "I have a boarding pass right here. This says I'm going to Winnipeg. I am going to Winnipeg! It's your job to get me to Winnipeg. Now - get me to Winnipeg!"

She responded with a tone of condescension, "I'm sorry Sir, you won't be going to Winnipeg tonight. As you know, this is a weather-related delay and there is nothing we can do about the weather. So, this is what I can tell you - you won't be going to Winnipeg tonight."

The customer stepped closer to the counter and shook his finger at the service agent. He loudly said, "Don't you tell me where to go!" (Actually, she had told him where he wasn't going.) "It's not your job to tell customers where to go. It's your job to get them where they're going. Get your manager out here. I want to talk to somebody who can make a good decision. I don't need a robot to tell me what I already know!"

Again, the agent apologized and tried to explain, "I'm sorry Sir, there is really nothing we can do. You need to understand. I could bring my supervisor out, but she'll tell you the same thing I'm telling you. You aren't going to Winnipeg tonight."

The angry customer stepped up on the luggage scale beside the counter. He was now face to face with the service agent.

His language became foul and his voice got louder than ever. He shouted, "Who the hell do you think you are? I paid good (expletive) money to fly with your airline. You had better find something (expletive) intelligent to say pretty quick. I am tired of your stupidity."

The agent made an effort to calm the outraged customer. She said, "I'm sorry, Sir, we have a policy that states we will not tolerate the use of foul and inappropriate language. If you continue to talk this way and yell at me, I will have to call security."

He shouted back, "Go ahead. Call security, maybe they'll get me out of this airport."

He had lost it!

The agent turned away and said, "I'll get my supervisor."

Meanwhile, the agent at the front of the line I'm in is working hard to handle his line of customers. We are all busy staring at the drama in the other line. (We may not want to be in a fight, but we are always willing to watch one)

As soon as the young man's computer was up and running, he turned to the customer in front of him and said, "Thank you for being patient. Now, let's see what we can do. Could I see your boarding pass? Oh, and I see you are headed for Halifax? The next available Flight is tomorrow at 2:30 PM. What would you prefer to do? Would you want to stay in Toronto overnight or should we try to get you out to Hamilton or another close airport for possible flights from there?"

The customer immediately asked, "Are you paying for a hotel if I stay in Toronto overnight?"

The agent calmly said, "If I could, I would pay for everyone in the airport. What I can do is give you a list of hotels and you can choose the one that best suits your needs. Or, you could consider bussing to another airport and we'll do our best to get you out of there. What do you think?"

"Would you prefer to stay in one of these hotels? Or, would you rather be bussed to an alternate airport?"

"It's your choice. What do you think? Stay in Toronto or go to another airport?"

"I can help make arrangements either way. Just let me know what would be best, staying or going?"

The customer hesitated and then said, "Put me on a bus to Hamilton. What are the flight choices out of there?"

The agent showed him three flight choices and got him booked for the next day.

Then, he asked, "Could you just step aside until we get 20 to 25 people to put on a bus with you? Then we'll have you on your way."

The customer thanked him and stepped aside. He immediately turned to the next customer and said, "Thank you for waiting. Let's see what we can do for you."

And so, it went! When I stepped up, I immediately said, "Can I see that list of hotels? What time can I get out of here tomorrow?"

Before I knew it, I was booked on an alternate flight and calling the hotel of my choice on my cell phone.

Meanwhile, back to the customer who was going to Winnipeg. The service agent's manager has come out to help. She reiterates the rule about foul and inappropriate language. He responds by telling her, "Go stuff yourself. I want some service, and nobody is listening. What the (expletive) are you going to do for me? This is ridiculous!"

Just out of curiosity, I started to keep track. Our service agent handled 17 of us before they were able to manage "Mr. Winnipeg" and get him headed to a hotel. My thoughts went to how differently the two service Agents approached similar customers. What did I just see? I was intrigued by the impact of applying a few simple strategies. What were the customer service strategies that impacted this experience?

1. **Get off to a good start**
2. **Ask instead of tell**
3. **Demonstrate empathy and avoid apology**
4. **Offer choices options and alternatives**
5. **Avoid defensiveness and explain why**
6. **Manage vocabulary**
7. **Focus on what can be done instead of what can't be done**
8. **Talk about what's next instead of what's past**

I couldn't help but wonder what would have happened if she had tried asking for the behaviours she wanted, instead of telling the behaviours she didn't want. I believe that for him, customer service is a challenge. For her, customer service may be a chore!

Setting limits and boundaries for yourself and your customer

Sometimes, people become emotional and make unreasonable and/or inappropriate demands. A very small proportion of our customers may even swear, yell, threaten or otherwise try to frighten and intimidate us.

It is important to stay calm, neutral, objective and always professional. As challenging as it is, we need to work hard to not catch this highly contagious behaviour. It is so critical that we don't imitate or respond negatively to such emotion. We need to clearly set limits and boundaries within which to work positively and productively.

Shared respect is the key to setting these limits and boundaries. Consider these responses to help define limits, set respectful boundaries and plan assertive responses when providing customer service.

Examples:

"The best way for us to find a solution is for both of us to use respectful language. Could we start again and see what we can do to get moving in a good direction? Where can we start?"

"As soon as we are able to look at this objectively, I'm sure we can find out what it is we can do."

"Will you help me work on this positively?" "I find it difficult to do that when we are yelling at each other."

"Will you work with me on this?" "I realize you are frustrated, and we need to figure out what will work for you."

Try to avoid inflammatory responses such as:

"I don't have to deal with you when you swear."

"You are not going to get anywhere with that behaviour."

"We have a zero-tolerance policy for foul language."

"If you continue to yell and swear, I will hang up the phone."

Chapter 4

Do You Have Your Receipt?

Customer service in the retail industry has become very challenging. Customers are often in a hurry. They have researched before they shopped. They know what they want and how much they will pay. They have compared products online, and decisions may be made before they even come into the shop. They are fully "Googleized." They ask a question and expect an answer. Same old, same old just isn't working anymore.

I have seen the impact of this on a number of occasions.

I was in a shoe store, not long ago. I was looking for a good pair of runners. I found the kind I like. They were there in size 6 and size 9. I need a 7 or an 8.

I picked up the size 6 and approached the customer service representative. I asked, "Do you have these shoes or something like them in a size 7 or 8?"

His reply was succinct, "I'm sorry," he said, "All we have is out there."

I was taken aback as he walked away. Could it be there is nothing similar, or something in another location? I wasn't sure what to do. I really didn't feel like looking again or looking further in that store. I put the shoes down in the wrong place to punish them for lack of service. On my way out of the store, I met a friend. I told her, "No use looking for shoes here. They never have anything in our size." We quickly left the store.

Any attempt at customer service may have kept me interested. I could have explored other possibilities. Negativity and lack of effort to provide service sent me on my way.

I watched a mother and daughter come into a store to return a sweater. The sweater was a Christmas gift as the mother explained, "My daughter got two of the same sweaters and we want to return it."

The salesperson immediately asked, "Do you have your sales receipt?"

The mother explained again that the sweater was a gift and the person who gave it to her lives out of town.

The salesperson replied, "We can't give a refund unless you have a receipt."

The mother became agitated and said, "Would you keep two of the same sweaters? Who wants two sweaters that are exactly the same?"

The salesperson replied, "I understand and I'm sorry. We have a policy that says we don't give refunds without the receipt. There is nothing I can do."

The mother shouted, "This is ridiculous, I want to talk to a manager." Other customers were watching and listening.

The salesperson went to the back of the store. Minutes later she came back with another person who introduced herself as the store manager. She approached the mother and daughter and asked, "Could I help explain the situation?"

The mother raised her voice and said, "My daughter got two of the same sweaters for Christmas. All we want to do is return one. Your staff tells us that you won't give a refund without a receipt. I don't have a receipt - it was a gift. You can see it is still in the gift box from your store. What more do you need?"

The manager looked at the sweater and said, "You're right, this is from our store and it was very popular for Christmas. What we can do is offer a credit for the amount of the sweater. Your daughter could choose another item in the store and we can apply the credit to the new purchase. Would that work?"

The mother said, "That would be great. We shop here all the time, why didn't your salesperson tell us that?"

Her question is a good question. Sometimes we get so focused on what we can't do we forget to tell customers what we can do. There is no value in telling customers what they should have done. And, the apology wasn't helpful. Asking instead of telling generally gets better results. Positive words engage customers positively. Negative words engage customers negatively. Word choice is so important in customer service.

What were the customer service strategies that impacted this experience?

1. **Get off to a good start**
2. **Demonstrate empathy and avoid apology**

3. **Focus on what can be done instead of what can't be done**
4. **Manage vocabulary**
5. **Move from formal to friendly**

"I want to talk to a manager"

Some customers feel that they have to go "higher" in the chain of command in order to get results. Discuss with your supervisor in advance how you will handle this. It is important that customers don't feel they have been given the "run around."

Example:

Customer (yelling):

> *"Get somebody out here who knows something. I want to talk to your supervisor!"*

Response:

> *"Of course, you can speak to the supervisor. He'll be available in about 15 minutes. In the meantime, let's see if there is anything we can get started on."*

Or

> *"My supervisor is here. She is excellent at handling these kinds of challenges. Let me call her for you."*

Or

> *"You're right – sometimes is it better to get a supervisor's perspective. I can have him call you as soon as he comes in or I could check with _________, who is also experienced with these situations."*

Always make your supervisor your positive support. Avoid statements like:

> *"My supervisor won't tell you anything different."*
>
> *"You can talk to my supervisor if you like, but he/she has to follow policies just like me."*

Chapter 5

Of Course, I Have an Appointment!

Sometimes, customer service is all about shared information. When we are working from a different understanding we end up with barriers to communication.

This was very clear to me recently at my doctor's office.

An elderly man entered the office and approached the reception desk. He said to the receptionist, "My name is Earl Smith - I have an appointment at 11:15 this morning."

The receptionist looked at her screen and said, "Let me see." After a minute of checking her appointment list, she looked up and said, "I'm sorry, I don't have an appointment for you this morning. Are you sure you made an appointment?"

The man looked confused and said, "Of course I made an appointment. Do you think I would come all the way over here on two different buses if I hadn't made an appointment? I have it on my calendar... look again."

The receptionist opened her screen again and said, "I'm looking at the whole day of appointments and you aren't on the list. Are you sure you have the right day? This is November 12th. What day do you think it is?"

The man was getting agitated now and replied, "Listen, lady, I may be old but I'm not stupid. I know what day it is, and I know when my appointment is. Let me talk to the doctor. She will straighten this out."

The reply he received did nothing to diffuse his agitation. She told him, "You can't talk to your doctor without an appointment. Do you want to phone and leave a message for her to call you back when she has a break?"

Fortunately, at this point, a co-worker came over and intervened. She asked, "Are we looking at today's appointment list?"

The old man replied, "Yes, and this nincompoop thinks I don't know what day it is, or what day my appointment is. She probably thinks I am old and demented. I made the appointment for today and I'm here for my appointment."

The co-worker simply said, "Let's see what we can do... Doctor Addy has an opening at 12:15. Could we fit you in at 12:15? Would you like to have a coffee while you are waiting?"

He didn't want to give up easily and asked, "Did you give somebody else my 11:15 appointment?

She quickly said, "We may have made a mistake, can we fit you in now at 12:15? Should I get a coffee for you?"

He shrugged and said, "I guess that will work. The next bus isn't until 2 o'clock anyway. I might as well be waiting here."

She smiled and said, "You're welcome to wait here until your bus arrives. Coffee is always on. I'm really sorry we couldn't find your appointment when you came in."

He sat down with his coffee and picked up a magazine.

What happened? It is so important in customer service to focus on what can be done instead of what can't be done. It is important to avoid any blame - especially directed at the customer. Suggesting to a customer that they may not be truthful or that they made a mistake is only going to lead to defensiveness. In customer service, customers are not interested in learning that they caused a problem. They are interested in the solution. Social skills are often helpful in bridging difficult customer service interactions sometimes you can change a negative to a positive by connecting in a social way with a customer.

What were the customer service strategies that impacted this experience?

1. **Get off to a good start**
2. **Demonstrate empathy and avoid apology**
3. **Connect on a personal basis**
4. **Focus on what can be done instead of what can't be done**
5. **Move from formal to friendly**

When is it a good idea to apologize?

- ✓ After you have found a solution
- ✓ When you have caused a delay or problem
- ✓ When you can be sincere about it

At the end of an interaction, if a solution has been found, you may be able to say:

"I'm sorry that caused such a delay."

Most people will respond with:

"That's okay."

Chapter 6

What If I Just Can't Pay My Bill?

When customer service reaches into the customer's wallet or bank account, there is often a very emotional investment. When a city, town or municipal government tries to collect overdue tax or utility bills, it calls for some exceptionally fine-tuned customer service skills.

Imagine providing customer service on the phone for this caller. The dialogue goes like this:

Caller:

"I just got a notice from the town saying that if I don't pay my bill in full by November 22nd, you'll cut off my water. What is that all about? I have 3 pre-school children and an elderly mother living with me. Don't you guys care about the people who live in this town?"

Customer Service Representative:

"Thanks for calling. Let's see what we can do to get this resolved. Could you confirm your address for me, and I'll look it up right away?"

Caller:

"You have caller ID - you can probably look up my address. Or, are you too lazy to do that?"

Customer Service Representative:

"Could you just confirm your address to help me get started on resolving this with you?"

Caller:

"I'm at 123-17th St. You guys have been here before. You seem to enjoy cutting services off from people who can't afford to pay."

Customer Service Representative:

"Thank you and I can see your utility bill right here. It looks like the full amount is $386.00. The good part is that as long as you can pay $123.00 by November 22, we can keep the water on. The next payment of $127.00 won't be due until December 29. Let's look at what we can do to be sure the water stays on for you."

Caller:

"If you have any compassion at all, you will just forgive it until after Christmas."

Customer Service Representative:

"Wow! I wish I could forgive everybody's bills until after Christmas. What we could do is break it up into smaller amounts and still let you get started on catching up."

Caller:

"The town's idea of a small amount is probably bigger than I can afford."

Customer Service Representative:

"Let's talk about that. How much could you start out with? Can we get a schedule in place that will keep your services on and help you get this bill under control?"

Caller:

Well, maybe I could pay $15.00 online today and another $15.00 on Monday. Then on the 20th, I get paid and I can probably manage the other $100 then. But it is going to leave me pretty close for other bills."

Customer Service Representative:

"That would work. Do you think you could send a note confirming that? What I can do is move the second payment of $129.00 to January 5. Would that help? Should we plan now to start on it with smaller amounts?"

Caller:

"I need to think about that. I just need to keep the water on over Christmas. It is really hard to cover all the bills and still give the kids a Christmas."

Customer Service Representative:

"I get that! We'll do our best to work with you. Can we talk again after November 22nd to find out what will work best for you? And, could you send that note to confirm the three payments we've set out for November?"

Caller:

"Ok, thanks."

What looked like a very difficult situation was quickly turned around. Excellent customer service skills made the difference. This customer service representative didn't buy into the negativity, criticism or even the victim statements. She stayed focused on what can be done. She asked and engaged the customer/caller in finding the solution. She even worked very hard to get a commitment to moving ahead positively.

It works!

What were the customer service strategies that impacted this experience?

1. **Get off to a good start**
2. **Demonstrate empathy and avoid apology**
3. **Ask instead of tell**
4. **Focus on what can be done instead of what can't be done**
5. **Offer choices options and alternatives**

Don't take the bait

Sometimes, customers like to throw out emotional bait. in customer service, we must be careful not to "take the bait." we must stay professional and focused on the solution or resolution. we can accept the emotional information without judgment or comment. Using empathy and avoiding sympathy will help.

For example, this customer wanted to bring her children and elderly mother into the story. That is emotional bait.

Chapter 7

I'm Sorry, There Are Nothing but Early Morning Appointments

When we are busy, we often try to be more efficient in our customer service. But sometimes efficiency sounds to the customer like brusque or blunt. It is even interpreted as being brushed aside or pushed out of the conversation.

I called my Dentist's office to make an annual appointment for a check-up. The receptionist answered with enthusiasm and I explained, "I need an appointment for a check-up in the next month or so."

She replied, "Oh dear, we have very few appointment times left this month. All we have is early morning time slots and nobody wants those."

I was thinking that early morning sounds appealing, but if nobody else wants them then neither do I. I asked, "What about next month? I'm fairly flexible."

Her answer was not very encouraging. She said, "We are really busy in that month as well. There are some early mornings again or some late day ones. Not the best times for sure."

I was starting to feel frustrated. I asked about the following month and her answers stopped me in my tracks. She said, "I really don't want to book anything that month until I've been able to confirm the Dentist's holiday plans. He is going to a conference in the east and will add holiday time to the conference time. I'll have to wait until that is settled before I can take bookings." I hung up the phone without an appointment.

What happened to customer service? Should we assume that we know what the customer wants or doesn't want? Why do we tell people what we don't have or can't do when we could tell them what we have and what we can do?

Should we ask more questions to clarify what will work instead of telling people what doesn't work? Should we take time to offer options, choices and alternatives or should we just send people away empty handed?

This whole situation could be reframed. What if I had been told that early morning appointments would allow me to have my check-up and get on with my day? What if I thought early morning appointments had value and could be helpful for me and my Dentist? What if I could choose between early morning and late day appointments depending on my preference?

What a difference that would make.

What were the customer service strategies that could have impacted this experience?

1. **Get off to a good start**
2. **Demonstrate empathy and avoid apology**
3. **Focus on what can be done instead of what can't be done**
4. **Offer choices options and alternatives**
5. **Manage vocabulary**

Chapter 8

The Sign Says…

I hear some people bemoaning the challenging behaviour of their customers. I hear phrases like, "Can't they read?" Or "Why don't they follow the rules?" Or "Don't customers have any common sense?"

Quite often, these comments are related to behaviours in public facilities or public areas. One such complaint came from a recreation facility manager. He said to me, "I can't believe the mess that hockey parents leave behind after they watch their children's games. I'm sure they would expect their children to behave better than that."

When I asked for detail, he explained it this way. "They come to the rink to watch their children play. They bring their coffee and snacks to enjoy. When they leave, they leave their cups, wrappers, napkins, Kleenex and stir sticks under their seat and walk away." "Why can't people just pick up after themselves?"

I empathized with him and asked a simple question, "Where are the garbage cans?"

He responded without hesitation. "There are two huge garbage cans at either end of the ice. They have to walk right by them to get to the exits."

I tried to speak from a customer perspective. I said, "I have been a hockey parent. I kind of understand. When we are watching our children play, our whole focus is on our children. We drink our coffee and eat our snacks. We just don't want to miss anything as we walk down to your garbage cans. So, we tuck our garbage in behind our feet and plan to pick it up later. But… then our children win, we race down to cheer and celebrate the win. We completely forget about our garbage."

There is an interesting perspective to this. When we make it easy for our customers to behave well, they will. When we make it difficult for customers to behave well, they won't behave well. What can we do?

This facility manager was so innovative. He went out, purchased 10 large plastic garbage cans and placed them strategically around the spectator stands in the rink. Just to add to the appeal, he took them to the junior high school nearby where he asked the art class to "artistically graffiti" the cans and sign their names to their work.

What a difference it made. Spectators talked about, complemented, pointed out and best of all, they used the garbage cans. Sometimes they would even walk a distance to place their garbage in the garbage can painted by children they knew.

It worked! There was much less garbage left behind and the cleanup was quick and simple. Indeed, they were soon able to replace the *"No Littering"* and *"Pick Up Your Garbage"* signs with new signs that read:

"Will you use our stylish new garbage cans and help us keep your facility clean and appealing to be a part of?"

Customer service is about working with our customers to get great results. What a difference a positive approach can make. We often get better results when we "ask" instead of "tell." We should always ask for the behaviour we want instead of telling the behaviour we don't want. Let's make it easier for our customers to behave well.

There are other examples of customer service messaging that is changing in tone and intent. The goal is always to ask for the behaviour you want instead of telling the behaviour you don't want.

An example is the often revised *"No Smoking"* sign.

The original sign with the *"No Smoking"* message was not getting the desired results.

It was changed to *"Absolutely No Smoking"* with the same outcomes.

The next change said, *"Absolutely No Smoking (In compliance with bylaw 674)."* Same result.

Their next effort was innovative, creative and definitely appealing to their customers. It was a bigger sign that said, *"Will you join your friends to enjoy your cigarette more than 3 metres from the door of this facility?"* It included a big pointing finger. When you looked where the sign was pointing, you could see a waving hand on the ashtray 3 metres away.

They are thrilled with the results.

One particularly busy area in an older part of the city was struggling with people parking in "no parking zones." The signs were clear and there were many "no parking" signs. Conversations with drivers established two things. First, they hadn't paid attention to the sign. Second, they were angry that they didn't know where to park.

Sandwich board signs in front of each business replaced the "no parking" signs. They give information and direction.

"Parking for the Candy Factory is one block ahead and one block to the right. Park behind the orange building."

"Parking for the Dine-In restaurant is one block ahead and one block to the left. Look for the signs."

Complaints were minimized and illegal parking decreased tremendously.

This is messaging for the customer service our customers expect. They don't want to be told what not to do. They want to work with you to achieve good service.

What were the customer service strategies that impacted this experience?

1. **Get off to a good start**
2. **Demonstrate empathy and avoid apology**
3. **Connect on a personal basis**
4. **Focus on what can be done instead of what can't be done**
5. **Offer choices options and alternatives**
6. **Manage vocabulary**

Chapter 9

You Forgot My Garbage Again!

I experienced a good customer service lesson while working with a woman in the Public Works Department of a small city.

When I met her, she told me the most difficult part of her job was handling the "garbage calls."

She went on to explain that the city picks up garbage every single day. She is tasked with handling the phone calls from people whose garbage was missed. She explained that everyday she gets 15 to 20 calls from people whose garbage did not get picked up. Upon further discussion, I learned that the garbage must be at the curb for pick up by 7:00 AM. It must be in the proper container and the container lid must be closed. Overstuffed garbage can not be picked up because the mechanical lift may not hold it and garbage will be spilled all over the street.

I agreed with her that all of it made good sense. I asked her to role play the typical customer interaction that happens in these calls. I agreed to play the role of customer. And so, it goes:

Customer:

"You forgot my garbage again. This is the 4th time you forgot my garbage. Do you guys do this on purpose?"

Service Provider:

"Did you have your garbage out by 7:00 AM?"

Customer:

"Of course, I had my garbage out by 7:00 AM. I've lived in this city for 40 years. Do you think that I don't know what time to put my garbage out?"

Service Provider:

"And was your garbage in the proper container?"

Customer:

"Of course, it was in the proper container. You gave me the container I know the system - green for compost, black for garbage, blue for recycle - do you think I'm stupid?"

Service Provider:

"And was the lid properly closed on the container? It can't be picked up if the container is overstuffed and the lid won't close."

Customer:

"Of course, I had the lid closed. Do you think I want garbage spilled all over the street?"

Service Provider:

"Well, I'll have to find out what can be done. Will you hold?"

Customer:

"I'll hold, but I don't have much time. How long will it take?"

Oh no! This was not going well. We always suggest asking questions for clarity. However, when we ask questions that cause the customer to be defensive or argumentative, we may want to reframe the questions. We also have to ask ourselves how the answers to those questions will impact the outcome of the discussion. We can't change what is already done. We have to move on to what's next and let go of what's in the past. We need to focus on what we can do instead of what the customer didn't do. Finding blame doesn't change the service we provide.

With some help from the group we were working with, we worked hard to change the discussion and interaction. We role played it again with a new positive approach:

Customer:

"You forgot my garbage again. This is the 4th time you forgot my garbage. Do you guys do this on purpose?"

Service Provider:

"Thank you for calling us so early. It really helps when we get the call early in the day. Could I just confirm your address?"

Customer:

"Yes! I'm at 274 Englewood Crescent."

Service Provider:

"Thanks for that. There are a couple of choices when this happens. Could I explain those to you?"

Customer:

"Of course, get on with it!"

Service Provider:

"Is it possible that you just have a small amount of garbage that could wait for the next pickup date? We have come to recognize that citizens are recycling more and composting more and that means less garbage every week. If it can wait, I'll put a note on the route plan to be sure it gets picked up on your next pickup date."

Customer:

"Of course, I didn't have much garbage. I care about reducing garbage as much as you do. I just don't think I should be missed as often as you miss my garbage. I pay for this service!

Service Provider:

"Of course, you do. I do have another option. I could give you a pass code and it would allow you to take your garbage to the landfill at no cost. In fact, if you have something else you wanted to take to the landfill, you could include that in the trip. Get rid of it for free."

Customer:

"Give me the number and I'll see."

Service Provider:

"The number is 13764. You can use this number anytime in the next 30 days."

Customer:

"I'll just haul my garbage back in for now and think about it."

Service Provider:

"I'm glad you called. We welcome the feedback. We do our best, but we know that sometimes things happen, and we try to always improve."

Customer:

"I guess nobody is perfect. Thanks for the suggestions."

What a difference! We followed up on the new approach for the next 12 months.

There was a concern that there would be a "rush" on the landfill. As it turns out, she gives out about 17 to 20 pass codes per month. Only 3 or 4 get used. Most citizens simply wait for the next pickup date. After all, people take pride in having less garbage.

As an addition to her conversation, she now keeps the actual number of the reduction in tonnes of garbage that the city delivers to the landfill. She often gives the number to customers and then thanks them for contributing.

She also noted that a number of her regular callers (Who may have been late getting their garbage out) was reduced significantly.

Calls are handled more quickly. The anger and defensiveness has been diffused. People are hearing the options and taking action. The discussions around blame and responsibility are gone. And, the job is less exhausting.

What were the customer service strategies that impacted this experience?

1. **Get off to a good start**
2. **Demonstrate empathy and avoid apology**
3. **Connect on a personal basis**
4. **Ask instead of tell**
5. **Explain why**
6. **Focus on what can be done instead of what can't be done**
7. **Talk about what's next instead of what's past**
8. **Offer choices options and alternatives**
9. **Manage vocabulary**
10. **Move from formal to friendly**

Chapter 10

The Customer Service Your Customers Expect

All of these stories demonstrate the changing nature of customer service. When customers change, customer service providers need to change as well. Old habits, old approaches and things we've always done just aren't meeting the expectations of the new customer.

Are we ready to provide the customer service our customers expect?